FIFTY MOSQUITOES

D.L. WARD

STORIES BY NUMBERS

ISBN (paperback): 978-1-7395559-0-0

ISBN (ebook): 978-1-7395559-5-5

Published by: Stories by Numbers

www.dlward.co.uk

For Iva, my fellow mosquito slayer.

FRIDAY 28/9/2012

11.30 pm

A vague sense of trepidation hit my stomach at the baggage reclaim, and it wasn't just the typical 'Where's my case?' jitters. This would be the longest holiday Claire and I had been on and our first with another couple. Claire got on well with Roger when they met last Christmas. Everyone always likes him. At first. She was thrilled when Roger invited us to stay, but something seemed a bit off. He practically begged me to come, trying to pull various emotional levers. Then, when I told him we would, he seemed almost giddy with relief. This desperation wasn't like him. I hope the trip goes well. Roger has this uncanny ability to make everybody feel at ease and get on well. He also has a tendency to catastrophically fuck things up.

That said, the trip is going well so far. Korean Air was smooth; great service, a good selection of films on the in-seat screen, and the food was decent too. I had bibimbap, a kind of rice, veg and meat mashup. Tasty. The airport was efficient, we passed through passport control, baggage collection and customs in no time. Was hoping for a slightly fancier visa stamp, but can't have it all I guess.

Roger greeted us at the airport and after some hugging whisked us over to a luxurious bus with only three seats in the row, footrests, cupholders and even USB chargers. The chairs were even comfier than the ones on the plane. Claire pushed past me to take the window seat, insisting she wanted to take in the view, then fell asleep after five minutes. Standard. Fortunately, she slumped down giving me an unobstructed view. It was more developed than I had thought it would be. In fairness, I knew it was reasonably developed—I'd seen Roger's photos on fb. But I couldn't get the misplaced image of farmers bending down in waterlogged paddy fields wearing conical hats. When I commented on this to Roger, he said, "That's Vietnam, you twat."

After some time I too must have fallen asleep as I was rudely awakened by Roger slapping me on the chops to get me off the bus. Claire struggled to wake up and dozed back off the moment we got in the taxi to Roger's place in Gunpo, a satellite city of Seoul.

His apartment is pretty much as he described it, a rather lacklustre vinyl-floored box room with a double bed, some tacky display furniture and a TV on a wobbly old computer desk. Oh, and the washing machine is in the bathroom. Roger says that all bathrooms in Korea are like this, with tiled floors, etc. He calls it a wet room and pointed out how easy they are to keep clean. "You can just shower everything down," he said at least three times. Pretty sensible to be fair, but his is pretty crowded, what with a hefty washing machine taking up a quarter of the space. Not sure about showering that down.

Roger headed over to his Missus' place nearby with his stuff and left us to unpack, shower etc. before coming back at 8ish, his lady friend in tow. Her name is Bohyeon (sp?) and she seems very nice. Not sure how an ugly git like him has pulled such a looker, but I suppose his personality's not so bad, he's my best mate after all. They took us to a heaving restaurant, called 'Sorae' (apparently it's a chain) with these strange chimney/ventilation pipe things hanging down from the ceiling over a grill. Took our seats and Bohyeon ordered for us. The waiter bought lots of random little side dishes including 'kimchi' (pickled spicy cabbage. Unexpectedly red.) and some other stuff the names of which I don't remember. Then, lastly, they brought several large slabs of raw brown, marinated pork which Bohyeon cooked on the grill for us. It was delicious, especially dipped into this red spicy sauce they served with it. Apparently some kind of bean?

We had a few glasses of beer each, and shots of the local liquor 'soju', which tasted a bit like vodka but sweeter and less harsh. Supposedly, it's notorious for its hangovers. The beer wasn't that great, to be honest. At the end, we didn't even have to leave a tip, as there's no tipping culture. Seems fair enough as Bohyeon did all the cooking, so why should we tip anyway?

Claire was flagging, so after a short walk around the area, and popping into the local (absolutely massive) supermarket for some fruit we headed back here. She's asleep as I type this. It's still mild here—I'm sitting in my T-shirt and shorts with the window wide open. Glad Roger told me to bring some as I wasn't expecting this. Makes a nice change from England, where our September threatens to collapse right into winter. There's still quite a lot of insects about. "Wing-ed cunts" as Roger would have it. I just heard the pitiful whine of a mosquito near my ear. Hope we don't get bitten tonight, I don't want to get Japanese Encephalitis. Anyway, that was much more than I was planning on writing for today. Bedtime methinks.

Thought for the day: Why do they make us pull down the window shutters on planes at night time, and at other times insist that we open them?

SATURDAY 29/9/2012

1 am

Bastard. I'd just dozed off when one of them flew right past my ear. Instinctively, I tried to swat it and ended up slapping myself on the ear. This in turn made me kick out and, well, kick Claire. She's currently got the hump, and I don't think I can get back in bed safely until she's sound asleep.

1.10 am

Went to the bathroom and the cheeky shit was perched right on the mirror, all plump with our blood. Ripped off a piece of bog roll and whacked it. Don't know how such a small insect can hold so much blood. Claire's gone back to sleep so I'm going to join her.

5 am

It seems there's more than one. Fuckers. Closed the window. Should have realised that was an error.

. . .

11 am

Claire seems to have forgiven me, or at least forgotten that I woke her up. Cereal for breakfast. About to shower, waiting for Claire to get out. She got bitten several times last night and isn't best pleased.

Jet lag isn't as bad as I feared it would be. Feeling reasonably fresh.

12.30 pm

Came out of the shower and Claire had opened the window. Feel like a right muppet. Claire opened the windows on the right-hand side, whereas I had opened the ones on the left last night. The difference is that behind the ones on the right, there's a mesh to keep the little sods out. Fortunately, I don't think she even realised I had the window open last night, and even if she did, she hasn't said anything.

Anyway, lesson learned. The insect mesh seems to be working well enough. Though it has one or two small holes, it's effective enough to keep in one mosquito which was trying to escape. I tried to 'help' it by pushing it through one of the holes, mangling its little body in the process. If it wasn't dead, it would have learned a valuable lesson. Going out now.

10.45 pm

A good first day in Korea. Fantastic weather. Roger and Bohyeon met us at the apartment. Roger managed to procure us a pre-paid cell phone. It's absolutely battered but capable of making and receiving calls, so we can keep in touch with them easily enough. We strolled over to a little restaurant near the apartment called 'Noodle Tree'. I wasn't feeling too adventurous food-wise, so I had something called 'omurice', basically rice wrapped in an omelette. I tried some kimchi again.

It's OK actually. Not as spicy as people have been telling me, but definitely as smelly. There was also a sweet yellow radish, which I can only assume is dyed somehow, as that yellow looked rather unnatural. Fortunately, it tasted quite nice. Claire had 'tonkatsu', which is like a pork escalope with a special sauce, not completely removed from barbecue sauce. After that, we headed over to Dangjeong subway station. Alongside it is a pretty park with some tennis nets, a basketball court and an artificial mountain replete with a waterfall. Weird.

My Dad, who visited Seoul ten years ago, had described it as an endless concrete jungle with hardly any green spaces, but so far, on the bus and walking around, we've seen quite a few. Bohyeon tells us that local governments are trying to create nicer spaces for their citizens, even providing outdoor exercise and stretching machines. A nice contrast to our local park back home, which is full of abandoned trolleys and dog shit.

The subway station was also pretty new. I nipped into the bathroom (which was free – London take note!) for a slash. There must have been a dozen mosquitoes in there too. Killed one just near the urinal, and another by the sink. I don't remember ever seeing so many mosquitoes before. Washed my hands thoroughly though, so don't worry.

The first stop of the day was at the Seoul National Cemetery. I wasn't really sure why they were taking us there, to be honest. Seemed like a strange place to start. In fairness, the cemetery was a peaceful, almost picturesque place. More than 165,000 bodies are buried there, marked in the green fields by small grey tombstones with artificial flowers, which looked more tasteful than it sounds. There are also memorial tablets for another 102,000 missing in action. With the sun beating down on us, it was far from an eerie place, but instead a sad reminder of the division of Korea, and the millions of lives lost in a fruitless battle. It seems all the more shocking when you think of the Cold War context of the Korean War, and how unnecessary it all was/is.

Bohyeon led us towards one of the fields, each marked with a large sign so that people might find their relatives. We walked right into the field, the graves laid out in perfectly symmetrical rows, and up to one of the graves. It was that of her grandfather, who died as the UN and South Korean forces reclaimed Seoul. He was 26 and left behind his pregnant wife, who months later gave birth to Bohyeon's mother and twin sister. The family come here every year on his 'Death Day' to honour him. We left Bohyeon for a few minutes of quiet prayer or contemplation, and when she caught up with us we headed back to the subway line. Claire took dozens of photos at the cemetery on her new SLR. She got some really good shots.

The next stop was an area called Myeongdong, which seems to be one of the shopping hubs of the city. The two girls went off shopping, but me and Roger didn't fancy it, so we sat in a coffee shop called 'Coffee Bean'. Pretty nice coffee there, although I'd rather have gone to an independent café. Roger tells me there are not so many around this area, but part of me suspects he was just being lazy. Whilst we had some time alone, I thought I'd try to get Roger to open up. He never shares his true thoughts or feelings in a group. It doesn't fit his showman/perfect host/all round centre-of-attention persona.

I wanted to know more about him and Bohyeon and if he was thinking about ever coming back to the UK. He's been in Korea for four years now. However, beyond briefly saying that Bohyeon had 'changed his life', he was slightly circumspect, not answering my questions seriously. He complained about the lack of career development in Korea, but when I asked him about his long-term plans, he just told me he wanted to do a marathon. He said he has been running regularly and usually does a 10km run every weekend. It was hard to reconcile this with the Roger I remembered from university who used to chain-smoke rollies. I don't remember him ever doing any exercise in the three years we spent together in Leeds. I tried to get him back onto the topic of a possible return to the UK, perhaps even joined by Bohyeon. I suggested he could do a PGCE but he dismissed the idea. He seemed to think that Bohyeon would find work easier than he would and generally seemed pessimistic about his prospects back in the UK. I'm not sure what's behind his pessimism. He's so confident and outgoing in most respects but doesn't seem to have much faith in his abilities or future. When I tried to boost his self-esteem and compliment him, he just brushed it off, instead telling me how great I was for coming over to visit. I used that as an opportunity to ask what had prompted his invite and he seemed almost defensive, saying that he just missed me, and asking if he needed another reason. It seemed he was holding something back. I explained I just thought that there might have been some other reason, but he said there wasn't. The two of us fell into a slightly uncomfortable silence, and I let it hang, hoping that in due course he'd say his piece. He was just about to speak when the girls arrived. Whatever he was going to say remained unsaid as Claire showed me her purchases.

She had splurged about £50 at a cosmetics shop, including buying thirty mask packs which I already doubt she'll ever use. Laden with the ladies shopping, which they had foisted upon us, we had a quick walk around the area. It's a crowded, lively area, with hundreds of shops, cafés and various other services, from novelty photo booths to 'DVD rooms'. Apparently, young couples often go to these DVD rooms, watch a DVD and maybe have sex. Private space is at something of a premium here as most young people still live with their parents right up until marriage. Claire then put her foot right in it by asking Roger and Bohyeon if they ever visit DVD rooms, at which point Roger cast her dagger eyes and

Bohyeon's face flushed a bright shade of fuchsia, and we walked on in a somewhat awkward silence for a few minutes.

Myeongdong is populated by various figures in character suits, from Mario & Mickey to Garfield and Snoopy, the latter two advertising a 'Cat Café' and 'Dog Café' respectively. Hoping to break the social impasse that had developed, I suggested we go and see what a Cat Café was. It was exactly how it sounded, a café with lots of cats in it. We spent a good hour there while Claire and Bohyeon fawned over the felines.

The café had been designed with plenty of nooks to hide away and sleep as well as scratching surfaces and a range of toys for customers to play with the occupants. With a steady influx of people to pet and feed them, some of the cats had understandably ended up being a bit spoilt. There's also a clear pecking order, with one fat, grey cat clearly ruling the roost, whom Roger nicknamed "The Godfather". Another of the cats was a bit mental, maybe on heat, and ran around, jumping on and off the cats' elevated walkways squawking, growling and mewing pitifully. It had wild green eyes the colour of pine needles, and just as sharp. Eventually, it hopped into one of Bohyeon's shopping bags and stayed there until we left. Claire took countless photos. I have to say I'm usually more of a dog person, but I'll admit the cats were pretty cute.

Post Cat Café, we headed back to the streets. The girls dragged us into this big shop called Kosney's selling all sorts of fancy tat, from scented candles to high-end earphones. Roger and I soon escaped and munched on some street food outside. I had two chicken kebabs and managed to get sauce on my jeans. When Bohyeon and Claire joined us, we went and tried some other street food, including a kind of thick battered pancake filled with cinnamon, some nuts and raisins. Tasted amazing. Next, took a subway to the famous Gangnam. After visiting it, I still have absolutely no idea what the 'Gangnam Style' is. We did go to a very cool shisha café called 'Rainbow' and chilled out there for a while before heading home. Bohyeon and Claire barely smoked whilst we were there, but I enjoyed it. Probably not as much as Roger though, who ordered a second shisha after we'd finished the first. I didn't have too much of the second one as by then my throat was feeling a bit rough.

A lovely day was rather irritatingly capped off by a mini-swarm of mosquitoes in the room. I have absolutely no idea how they're getting in unless they are following us through the door. We'd closed the window earlier, so it can't be that. I went on a rampage for about twenty minutes and caught four with my bare hands. Needle-mouthed little pricks.

Thought for the day: Mosquitoes are one of the reasons I find it hard to believe in God.

SUNDAY 30/9/2012

4.10 pm

Bohyeon came and knocked on the door around ten. Both of us had been fast asleep, so I answered the door in a state of dishevelment. I have to say she's very attractive. She's about Claire's height, svelte, with shoulder-length black hair, and a smile to turn heads. She seems to treat Roger well too, tolerating his bad habits and his flaws. I love the bloke to bits, but I couldn't put up with him in a relationship, even if I were that way inclined. Anyway, she brought us coffee and pastries from the local bakery, called Paris Baguette.

Roger joined us as we were finishing breakfast, looking a bit sheepish, and the mood in the room darkened somewhat with his entrance. Claire thinks the two of them must have had a spat. I reckon she's right. Why else would Bohyeon come over rather than Roger? That's their business I guess. There was a spare pastry covered in cheese, sausage and some veg, so Roger made himself a quick cup of tea and munched on that, whilst the girls wittered on about one another's accessories. It was massively exciting obviously, and Roger and I shared a brief look and a smile that said it all for both of us. It reminded me how much I've missed him in the past few years he's been here. Anyway, Roger fed and watered, he and I grabbed the two suitcases we'd packed – one per couple and headed down the elevator. Us two walked in the lead, catching up on one another's opinions on the footy whilst the girls continued their conversation behind us. How is it that girls can bond so rapidly to the point of walking along arm-in-arm having basically just met? Me and Roger never walk like that and we've known each other for eight years.

The journey up to Seoul station didn't take too long, and we had enough time to get a few snacks for the train down to Gyeongju. With time to spare, we headed down to our train, an impressive-looking beast which reminded me somewhat of a Eurostar train. The train is called the KTX and is supposed to be Korea's equivalent of the Japanese Bullet trains. Claire was watching a YouTube video of a Discovery Channel documentary last night, and from the snatches I saw, it seems like quite a feat of engineering, with long tunnels built through mountains and traversing wide valleys. Roger had only been able to get two seats for the train, as originally they hadn't planned on accompanying us. He suggested that the two ladies take the seats. I wasn't sure if he made the suggestion as he was being a gent, or if secretly he wanted to avoid the wrath of Bohyeon for whatever it is he'd done to piss her off. Either way, I didn't mind too much, it was the right thing to do, and meant me and him could continue to catch up.

Fortunately, Roger and I were able to get two seats outside the main compartment of the carriage. These were flip seats, and Roger assumed that they were for whoever got there first, which fortunately appeared to be us. The train left on schedule, and shortly various people were embarking and disembarking. Two such people were an ageing couple, not quite elderly, but definitely heading that way: late 50s probably. By this time, we were alone in our sheltered little end-of-carriage alcove with the two of them. The woman seemed annoyed and was having a whinge about something, gesturing towards us but the husband gave her short shrift and she calmed down, laying down some newspaper and sitting on the floor in a huff. I made to stand up and give her my seat, but Roger caught my eye, shook his head gently, and then pointed at his mobile. A minute later, he sent me a message saying, "She just said, 'Foreigners shouldn't be able to sit instead of Koreans.' Stay put." I looked over and he winked at me whilst the woman sat there, continuing to sulk. After twenty minutes or so, Roger got up and gave her his seat, speaking in (what I assume to be) very good Korean. The woman, with a face contorted somewhere between mortification and satisfaction took it. When the snack trolley was wheeled by, her husband bought us each a beer and some packaged Korean sausages, whether out of gratitude or embarrassment, I have no idea.

That aside, the journey was reasonably uneventful as the Korean countryside swept past in a blurry tapestry of greens, browns and beiges; mountains interspersed by fields and the odd urban area. We finally got to Gyeongju KTX station two and a half hours after leaving Seoul.

From the train station, we boarded a bus taking us into Gyeongju. Claire and I boarded first, nabbing two seats near the back. There weren't any other seats, so Roger and Bohyeon had to stand. After a few stops, the seats in front of us became available. I called to the others to join us and Roger put his hand on Bohyeon's arm, but she immediately brushed it off. Roger called back that it was only a few more stops. Moments later, I saw Roger lean over to say something in Bohyeon's ear. She turned towards him, fury etched on her features and said something rapid in Korean. Roger tried to look composed but winced slightly. Even Claire had noticed at this point and under her breath said, "Trouble in paradise?". Just as she did, the bus broke suddenly, jolting us forward and making Roger stumble into Bohyeon. He must have trodden on her foot, because she yelped in pain, then shoved Roger away from her and turned her back on him. Roger sighed and then turned towards us. Claire looked out of the window to avoid eye contact. Roger grimaced and shrugged at me. I offered him a look of sympathy. But, knowing Roger, Bohyeon was probably justifiably annoyed with him.

We got off the bus five minutes later, the bus stop was close to two huge mounds rising up out of the ground, somewhat like big, grassy breasts. Bohyeon navigated us over to our guesthouse, which was called 'Homo Nomad Guest House'. I'm guessing they were going for homo as in Homosapien. That wasn't what me or Roger were thinking, but a sharp look from Claire reminded us we were being immature. Anyway, the place is pretty cool, its exterior walls painted with imitations of famous street art, including the Banksy where a guy is throwing a bouquet of flowers in place of a Molotov cocktail. We entered through a gate and were greeted by a nice lady who showed us into a beautiful traditional building, albeit with a few modern touches, including a communal kitchen equipped with all mod cons. The stairs and most of the furniture are all made of hardwood, and the décor includes a scattering of Korean antiques, knick-knacks and ornaments. Oh, and a random Bob Marley flag.

We were shown our rooms. We'll be sleeping on mats on the floor, which I'm not thrilled about, but we're told this is how Koreans traditionally sleep. Claire too is concerned in case a creepy-crawly decides to join us. The mats are reasonably thick, and Bohyeon tells us that many Koreans sleep on thinner mats, so there's something to be said for the small mercies permitted to tourists I guess. So that brings us up to where we are now. Roger and I are sitting in the lobby whilst the ladies are in our respective rooms. Claire has been napping for the past hour or so as the jetlag suddenly caught up with her, and Bohyeon is presumably avoiding Roger. I hope they resolve soon. It's going to become a bit uncomfortable otherwise. We're supposed to be going out in half an hour, so I'm going to have a read and I might have a word with him about it actually. Just caught a mosquito. Squished it on the screen.

10.40 pm

Once I saved the above, I washed the squash-quito (squozzie?) off my fingers and made Roger and I each a sachet of super sweet pre-mixed coffee. He was looking sorry for himself. I sat down opposite him and asked him what was going on with him and Bohyeon. He said it was nothing, just a few little things which had added up. She hadn't been happy with him smoking so much shisha the night before and was annoyed that we'd not had four seats on the train. She'd told him to get them booked earlier, but he had forgotten. Treading on her toes on the bus probably hadn't helped either. I told him to go upstairs and grovel. She'd probably just wanted some space. He'd given her that and she was now probably just waiting for him to apologise. He nodded, then sighed, slapped his legs and stood up and said, "Wish me luck." Instead, I said, "Just don't make it worse."

He laughed and toddled off to his room, leaving me to read the latest Adrian Mole book on the sofa.

Just after 6, Roger emerged hand in hand with Bohyeon, her looking slightly flushed, him with a big grin on his face. Good work. I made us all a cup of coffee and took one up to Claire, who was easy to rouse for a change, and then rejoined the now-at-peace couple.

Once Claire arrived downstairs with her camera and tripod in tow, we ventured out for dinner and a stroll. Back on the main road, we walked back towards the town, a load of grass mammaries on our right. Not far off, a squat stone building was illuminated in burning gold. Bohyeon tells us is the oldest observatory in Korea. Before we reached it, however, we turned left and over to a traditional gate surrounding a small park. Roger said the park is 'Tumulli Park'. Tumullis are the aforementioned grass breasts, standing twenty to thirty metres tall, marking the tombs of the Silla royals and aristocracy. The Silla Kingdom was one of the early Korean kingdoms.

We had a nice, dawdling stroll while Claire got some good photos, getting Bohyeon to model, a role that Bohyeon relished. Me and Roger were even harried into a few shots, but evidently, our modelling skills left something to be desired when compared to Bohyeon. Or maybe it's because we're not natives. Claire's such a photo-racist like that.

Our Tumulli Park experience was pleasant enough, and ended with a peek inside one of the Tumullis, which had been excavated and reconstructed to allow tourists inside for that tastefully-done 'this is what you would see if you were a buried Korean royal who wasn't already dead' experience. From there, we walked into town, stopping momentarily for a bit of photography faffing, but I'll let my darling Claire off as she got some very nice shots.

In town, we struggled to find anywhere good for dinner. Today is the main day for Chuseok (the Korean harvest festival) meaning many of the shops and restaurants were closed. We looked in at one restaurant with a cartoon squid on their sign. I was hoping for some meat if I'm honest but there didn't seem to be any on the menu. It looked a bit squidy and octopussy, and I'm more of a fish person. Fortunately, Roger doesn't eat seafood, so I was saved the experience of chewing on tentacles. Instead, Bohyeon and Roger took us to a small toasted sandwich chain that they like, called Isaac's.

Isaac's serves the toasted bread out of a window at the front of the store, which is basically a small kitchen, with two large square pans which cook everything. We all had a 'Ham

Cheese': white bread, a slice of ham, a square of fried eggs with sweetcorn cooked into the mix. As the ham and egg are fried, the slices of toast are coated with a special butter mix that Roger says is a secret recipe. Kiwi is definitely a part of it. Finally, the ham and egg are slid onto the bread, and a slice of processed cheese is placed on top. Despite its humble ingredients, it tasted fantastic. So much so that Roger and I both had another one. What's more, it's an absolute bargain – one sandwich costing little more than a quid.

Isaac's was right next to the cinema, which was showing 'Taken 2'. Roger's a Liam Neeson fan, and we'd all seen the original, so we decided to book tickets for that. Roger quickly headed up there whilst Bohyeon led us round the corner to a café, as the film wasn't due to start for another thirty minutes. In the café, the girls shared a waffle with cream cheese and a blueberry parfait, which made me a bit jealous that I'd already stuffed myself. The film was pretty good too; it's not going to get any Oscars, but it was fun, not too drawn out, and continued the story nicely. If I was an Albanian I probably wouldn't like it so much, but I'm not, so that's that.

Film done, we returned to the hotel. Definitely ate too much stodge today. Looking forward to more traditional Korean food tomorrow. Gonna end it here as need to catch up on my work e-mails, just to make sure there's nothing too urgent. Claire wants to use the computer after that.

_11.50 pm_

The bathroom is outside the main building, and several mosquitoes and a creepy-looking centipede were roosting in there. Roger says there's basically no chance of getting Japanese Encephalitis at this time of year, but I checked the maps of where people have contracted it, and there were some recent cases around here. I just have to kill them before they bite me. Bludgeoned three mosquitoes whilst brushing my teeth, but left the centipede alone. He wasn't trying to suck my blood.

Anyway, when I got back to the room, Claire was pissed off. She saw what I wrote about Bohyeon being very attractive. I think it's a bit unreasonable, as it was a statement of fact. I said, "Well, you're attractive too of course." This was apparently exactly the wrong thing to say as I had written, "Bohyeon's a very attractive girl," whilst omitting the "very" when talking about Claire. Then, a few minutes later, whilst trying to kill a mosquito, I accidentally elbowed her in the ribs. So now I'm in the doghouse. I eventually caught the little sod, but that did nothing to improve Claire's mood. Oh, and I've just been told that I'm typing too loudly, and been ordered back to bed.

Thought for the day: For some reason, I miss carpet.

MONDAY 1/10/2012

10.15 pm

This morning, headed out around 10 as we had a busy day planned. Walked to a nearby bus stop under Bohyeon's guidance. Stopped on the way at a local specialist bakery for some 'Gyeongju ppang'. The literal translation is 'Gyeongju bread,' small buns with a fairly thin crust, packed full of a sweet-tasting maroon paste, made from some sort of bean. Koreans seem to love beans. It's much nicer than it sounds though, and Roger bought us a box of twelve and we each had three for breakfast. The bus journey wasn't too long, and soon we were heading up a slope to a Buddhist temple called Bulguksa. Also from the Shilla period, it's one of the most famous temples in Korea, and it's easy to see why.

Despite the thronging crowds, it's a lovely place, with various shrines within the temple complex. The temple has been rebuilt and renovated using traditional materials and keeping any original parts they had. The paintings on the roof beams etc. are fantastic, and the whole place has a real charm. It may sound somewhat clichéd, but it really did seem to be a holy place. Roger was enthusing about the Buddhist iconography and telling me the meaning of everything. I have to say it was somewhat lost on me, but it's always entertaining seeing him get excited about something. He gets this slightly manic glazed look in his eye, smiling wildly, firing off sentences like a Gatling gun. Bless him. Whilst Claire was pottering around the gift shop for things for the folks back home, I played around with her camera in an area where there were piles of small stones stacked up, like little cairns. Roger says that these are 'stupas' and that they're an offering to the Gods.

Claire joined the rest of us and complimented me on some of the photos. Normally, she points out how I could make the photos better. I suppose her tips are working because one or two of the pictures were pretty artistic and she seemed pleasantly surprised too. I was quite chuffed. I was even more pleased to find out that she'd done half of my gift shopping. I'm rubbish at shopping, and I usually ask her advice anyway, so she just took it upon herself to do it for me! I was touched. She'd bought some jewellery for my Mum, my grandmother, and a wodge of postcards for us to send. Oh, and she sorted out my secret Santa gift for Dave from work, by picking up an imitation wooden sword. Dave's a bit of an anime geek, so he'll probably like it. Roger too, loved it, and dashed off to the gift shop, returning with two more swords, banging on about how "we must have sword fights" on the way up to Seokguram.

So, we walked up to Seokguram, with me spending the first ten minutes attempting to parry the blows of a suddenly child-like Roger who didn't tire from it all the way up. He's fitter than he looks. All the running and stopping smoking has done the world of good for him, and I expect Bohyeon has played a role in that. The path to Seokguram was nice. Quite steep, and soon the two girls were a fair way behind, but it went through a lovely wooded area, mostly following the natural slope, but sometimes turning into stairs.

Seokguram itself was well worth visiting. We had to queue

for a bit on a path which led to a cave. Then we entered this building at the mouth of the grotto and inside, behind a plate of glass was this beautiful statue of a seated, serene-looking Buddha in an ornately carved and tastefully lit chamber. It was unforgettable.

On the way back down, Claire was struggling a little bit with the steep slope and leant heavily on me as she took my arm and I helped guide her down the slope, catching her several times as she stumbled. Earned myself a few brownie points there. Once back down by Bulguksa, the path was no longer so steep. It was after two and now hungry, we walked down a small road lined with a few different restaurants, but Roger refused to go near them. It was evidently a slow day for most of them, and several of the owners stood in the doorways of their restaurants, beckoning us over in a mix of Korean and broken English. For whatever reason, this wound Roger up, whilst Bohyeon smirked at his irritation.

Eventually, we were passing a small restaurant with several people already sitting there, and a cat with a stump for a tail lingering around the entrance. Spying the cat, he exclaimed, "Lucky cat!" and went and sat at a table. Judging by what was left of the animal's tail, it wasn't all that lucky. Claire gave me her trademarked 'What the fuck?' look. I shrugged and followed Roger over to the table and took a seat opposite him, with our girlfriends sitting next to us. An exceedingly old lady came over and showed us a picture menu, followed by "Lucky" the cat, who strolled between our legs, to the cooing of the ladies. We ordered, with all of us choosing to eat Bohyeon's recommendation of 'dolsot bibimbap'. Roger headed to the bathroom, and whilst there, Claire asked Bohyeon, "Why was Roger so funny about choosing which restaurant we go to?"

"Roger doesn't like being told to do something and doesn't like people trying to get him to go to their restaurant.

He even hates it in shops when the sales assistants follow him around."

"The sales assistants follow people around here?" I said, "I'd hate that too."

"Yeah, it's really helpful actually," said Claire, who had already experienced shopping here. I kept quiet, but I could understand my friend's distaste for it.

Lunch was lovely. The old lady shuffled our food over to us, stooped at an almost 90-degree angle over the trolley. I don't know how she copes in the restaurant as she seems to be running it all by herself as manager, cook and waitress. The main dish was like a posh version of what I had on the plane. Dolsot bibimbap is a rice dish served with carrots, mushrooms, courgettes and bean sprouts with a bit of meat. This is all topped off with an egg. The dish is served in a hot stone bowl, meaning that the rice and other ingredients are still cooking. As the egg gets mixed in, a tasty crust of rice and whatever else forms on the side of the bowl. Finally, after laying all the dishes out, the old lady produced a tub, from which she gave each of us a dollop of a red chilli paste. Claire asked for none but instead received an extra-large spoonful. Something was lost in translation there. No real harm done as I switched bowls with Claire when the lady turned around.

Additionally, we were given the usual kimchi and a few other side dishes, plus two bowls of 'Doenjang jjigae', a bean-based broth with tofu in it as well. The whole lot was delicious, although I think Claire struggled with the spiciness a bit. As we tried to leave, the old lady had quite an in-depth conversation with Roger and Bohyeon that we didn't understand. She was very sweet.

We had not long left the restaurant, the old lady seeing us off at the door when something weird happened. As we walked up the hill back towards the bus stop, Roger pointed at a black car parked about fifty metres ahead of us. Two women were standing by the open boot, one an old lady with straight grey hair, one around our age who had a baby strapped in a carrier, leaning on her chest. She held the baby's head as she packed something into the boot. I lost sight of the older lady (maybe the other woman's Mum?) as she got into the car. The younger woman, I assume the baby's mother then put her baby into the backseat of the car. She was about 5'7, slim and like Bohyeon, had shoulder-length hair, but it was curled slightly at the end and dyed a deep red, beyond auburn, approaching the colour of red wine. I couldn't see much of her face as she was in profile, but clearly, Roger recognised her. "It's definitely her," he said to Bohyeon and then he shouted out, "Rose!"

The younger woman turned towards us, startled, then looked around in mild panic. Roger made towards her, hurrying his step, but as he did so, she hopped into the car. As Roger got towards the car, the reverse lights went on, and Roger was left knocking on the driver-side window as she reversed. He chased it half-heartedly as the car sped off towards the main road before turning right. Roger turned around to face us, throwing his arms up before walking over to us, fists clenched in frustration.

Bohyeon put her arm around him as he rejoined us, and he raked his shaggy hair with his hand, and said, "That was her." He was wide-eyed and pale. Bohyeon just nodded, clearly concerned. With hindsight, it wasn't the best time to start flailing around for a mosquito, but the instincts kicked in. Caught the bugger as well. I'm getting quite good at this.

The bus journey back was quiet. Claire asked if I had any idea what was going on, but I was clueless. We weren't able to get seats right next to each other either, so I let Claire have a seat, and stood next to her, whilst Bohyeon and Roger sat in the only two available seats at the back. They had a long, quiet conversation, and then Roger spent a while staring at his phone. Eventually, Bohyeon indicated to us that we should get off and they led us straight over to a small independent café, across the road from the observatory we had seen last night.

As we walked inside, Roger turned to us and said, "Look guys, I know that must have all been a bit odd, but I'm gonna explain everything, I just really need a coffee first." Roger spilt the beans (pun only slightly intended, and probably somewhat inappropriate, but it's been done now) as we sat there slurping our coffees and eating pastries.

The woman with the red hair was the ex-fiancé of a guy called Duncan, a good friend of Roger's, who had left Korea last year. Roger didn't want to go into details, but said that something major had happened and the woman disappeared. This Duncan had gone to ground, a complete state and didn't recover before leaving Korea a few months later. Apparently, he had spent his last few months before he left in a kind of drunken haze, hardly talking to anyone. Roger had seen him when he went back at Christmas, and he was still pretty miserable then, but when they had spoken recently, he had been doing better. As such, Roger hadn't been sure whether to tell Duncan that he had seen Rose, but ultimately, Bohyeon had convinced him that his mate deserved to know. Previously, Roger had suspected that Rose had committed suicide. I suppose that goes some way to explaining why Roger looked as though he'd seen a ghost. A ghost with a baby, at that! I just listened to what Roger said, unsure of whether he should tell Duncan. The way I saw it is that if Rose didn't want to be found, that was her prerogative. The popular opinion seemed to be against me though and even Claire chimed in that she thought Roger should tell Duncan, especially if the baby might be his, so I kept my thoughts to myself.

We went back to the hotel after the coffee. Claire and I sat in our room, Claire using the laptop whilst I flicked through the guidebook. Meanwhile, Roger and Bohyeon went to their room to call his friend and tell him what he'd seen. The UK is 8 hours behind Korea, so Roger must have spoken to him quite early in the morning. Can you imagine being told that your missing fiancé has turned up? With a kid? He must have spat his breakfast out.

Anyway, after an hour or so, Roger seemed to have collected himself enough to show us over to Anapji Pond. By the time we got there, it was after 6 pm and had just started getting a bit dark. The guidebook tells me that Anapji was, "constructed by King Munmu in 674 as a pleasure garden to commemorate the unification of the Korean peninsula under Shilla." Lots of historical relics have been found in the pond, and there were once several buildings around it for holding banquets and events. Nowadays, there are just a few of the traditional-style plinths with tiled roofs with raised corners. I like that style of roof, it's very elegant. Not sure how leak-proof they are though, and I bet the maintenance costs a few bob.

Anyway, it was all beautifully lit in rotating palettes of red/blue/purple and yellow/orange/red and Claire got a few nice photos, but the place was swamped with people, locals and tourists alike. Bohyeon told us that most of the tourism in Korea is internal tourism, i.e. Koreans travelling to other parts of Korea. However, she reckoned most of the people there were locals, out in force as today was still a national holiday: the last day of Chuseok. The only bad thing I can say about the place is that there were shitloads of moths and mosquitoes. Moths are bad enough, but since coming to Korea, I have decided that mosquitoes are my nemeses.

I didn't manage to kill any whilst we walked around the pond as it was too dark to see, but when I went for a slash, one descended upon my forearm for its dinner. Roger had told me that if you flex whilst they're sucking your blood, then their sucker gets stuck and they swell up and explode. I thought I'd try this, but when I went to wash my hands, I must have unflexed (is this a word?) and the little shit flew off. In fairness, it had grown to quite a large size, and I was able to spot it and batter the thing's brains (and my blood) out of it against the wall. I spied another one and smacked that too. I got a few odd looks from the Koreans in the bathroom, but I didn't care, I was doing us all a service. When I told the others of my exploits, Claire was a bit quiet, and Bohyeon gave me a funny look—got a high five from Roger though.

From Anapji, we headed back to the hostel, briefly winding our way through a maze-like pattern of flowerbeds, all of which were succumbing to autumn. Roger and I were talking about music and broke into an impromptu medley of Badly Drawn Boy songs. Claire joined in, and Bohyeon looked vaguely embarrassed. We stopped briefly at Cheomsongdae and Claire took some photos with her camera on a tripod before we finally headed back to Homo Nomad.

About to go to bed now. Had a rather nice day, even if that incident with the woman called Rose was all a bit odd. We skipped dinner but didn't feel that hungry after a big late lunch. Whilst brushing my teeth and whatnot, killed two more mosquitoes. I saw the centipede scuttling about as well. I wonder how he feels about the murder of the mosquitoes. Either appalled, indifferent or quietly pleased.

Thought for the day: I need to stop boasting about my mosquito massacring. I think the others, well, the girls anyway are starting to think it's a bit weird. Somewhat of an obsession. They might be right. Still, Claire has taken to spraying DEET all over herself and me. Stinks. I'd rather be bitten, although I appreciate the gesture.

TUESDAY 2/10/2012

9 pm

Today was slower paced than the past few. Toast for breakfast, then packing and brushing our teeth (during which I killed four mosquitoes. Prolific.). We took a train in the morning from Gyeongju to Andong, the next stop on our 'Cultural Tour' of Korea that Roger had planned for us. Unfortunately, we were left without seats again. I didn't mind too much, but Bohyeon and Claire took a seat at every opportunity they could when they were periodically vacated. Claire had a run-in with an old Korean lady who came and jabbed her several times in the side of the head. She could have at least said something to Claire, and I wasn't too impressed. Roger explained that elderly people are at the top of the social hierarchy, and whilst most are perfectly nice, some use it to get their way and generally push people around. Claire had been on the receiving end of one such tyrant.

Once in Andong, we dropped our bags straight at the hotel. Compared to our rather lovely guesthouse in Gyeongju, this place was a bit plain. On the plus side, it's cheaper, and en suite, meaning I no longer had to stumble downstairs and outside for the bathroom. These days I seem to pee more often at night. When I get back to England, I better get my prostate checked. The room has a computer, and Claire's on it now, sending e-mails back home.

Other than that, the only particularly interesting thing about the hotel is that the bed is circular. It's somewhat reminiscent of a 70s soft porn movie. Claire seems quite taken with our retro sleeping apparatus and even suggested we watch some porn later. Obviously, I think that's a great idea. What with jet lag etc. we haven't done it since getting to Korea, and I have to say that if I don't get some action soon, I might go a bit mad.

After allowing the girls a bit of time to freshen up, we headed out and ate lunch at a cheap place. I had another omurice with shrimp, and Claire had a rather bland-looking noodle dish. Andong has a festival going on right now, so we strolled through that. We happened upon a market area, which Roger tried unsuccessfully to circumnavigate, as we soon lost the girls to a stall of wooden masks and other handicrafts. Fortunately, they didn't want their sulking, killjoy boyfriends around, so we headed off on our own. There was plenty else going on at the festival, with a group of wisened old men doing a 'farmers dance' by the main stage, and several other things including masked dances from various other countries including Nepal and Thailand being performed at another stage. Roger, however, is never at his most comfortable in large crowds, and I saw he felt a bit uncomfortable, so suggested we move away from the crowds.

We walked without any particular destination in mind, along a road running parallel to a dammed river. The roadside was dotted with huge webs of big, bright yellow spiders. Roger picked up a twig and gently prodded a few, but they looked very poisonous, and I wanted no part in that. I nearly shat myself when one of them fell from its web and started running towards us. I'm not usually scared of spiders, but the ones at home don't look like literal hazard warnings. Once he'd stopped laughing, Roger gave up his arachnid bothering and we traversed the river using a zigzagging bridge. It had a traditional raised seating area, somewhat like a bandstand in the middle. After crossing, we continued up a hill to find a quaint, attractive mock-up of a traditional village. Roger pointed out how they were all raised from the ground, with underground stoves which heated the floors. We had a quick look about then made our way back on the same route.

Roger was curiously quiet right up until we reached the bridge, and when we got to the raised area, he took a seat, so I sat next to him. With his chin on his hand, he turned to me with this intense look in his eye and said, "I've been a naughty boy since I came here, Tom." I looked back at him, not saying anything, but he carried on staring at me for at least a minute before he continued.

In Christmas 2009, Roger returned to the UK for a holiday, having been in South Korea for just over a year. He was accompanied by Caroline, a stunning Japanese-American woman. She'd never visited the UK before and Roger was delighting in giving her a local's tour. Caroline seemed to have brought out a slightly humbler, more mature side in Roger that I hadn't seen in him. They were all loved up, so I was surprised when they broke up the following summer. Roger had told me things just weren't working. Today he told me the truth.

"I cheated on her. Every other weekend."

As he told me about it, he almost sounded like he was bragging. I challenged him on it, and he said he wasn't bragging, he was exposing himself. He'd been a cunt and he knew it.

Roger had been found out one weekend in a pub in Itae-won, Seoul's foreign enclave. He and Caroline had been playing pool and when she went to the toilet, an Australian girl came up to Roger and began laying into him. She was calling him an arsehole, bollocking him for not calling her, or even giving her the cab fare the next day. Supposedly, the two of them had fucked, but Roger barely remembered her. Unwisely, he said something to that effect and she lost her shit. She started yelling at him, unleashing a tirade of insults. Roger tried to apologise, but she wasn't having it, so he told her to fuck off. Caroline returned from the bathroom just in time to see the Aussie throw her drink in Roger's face. Unsurprisingly, Caroline had questions for Roger, and his face dripping with JD & Coke, he answered them truthfully. She broke up with him on the spot and he never saw her again.

Roger knew he deserved it, but that didn't stop the self-pity. According to him, he'd never felt so alone in his life and had something of an identity crisis. He even went to church. I had to laugh when he told me that. He's always said he's a devout agnostic with atheist leanings. Honestly, short of the Ayatollah, he's the last person I could imagine going to church, but apparently, he did. Some of the churches in Itaewon have English sermons, so he went to one of those hoping to do a confession to see if that relieved the burden of his sins. The only issue is it wasn't a Catholic church, but a protestant one, so there was no Confessional. He then tried to speak to a pastor, but it didn't give him the solace he needed. Instead, he felt judged, and when they said, "Jesus forgives", Roger felt patronised rather than absolved. I found it hard to buy into Roger's pity parade, so I told him forgiveness needs to be earnt, not just granted for acknowledging your wrongdoing. He had to make amends. This wasn't the first time Roger had cheated and after what happened when we were at university, he couldn't really expect my sympathy and I told him so.

He understood and wasn't expecting me to feel sorry for him, he just wanted to talk about it. According to him, he hadn't told many people about this, and certainly not that he'd been to church, as if that was the biggest thing he had to be embarrassed about.

Ultimately, Jesus' alleged forgiveness didn't mean much to Roger and Caroline wouldn't speak to him, so he'd been unable to earn hers. Guilt had a hold on Roger, and for months after, he was miserable. He decided not to be with anyone for a while. He felt that if he didn't have the self-control not to cheat, he shouldn't be in a relationship at all. Finally, he was saying something I could agree with, even if I still couldn't make sense of it. He had seemed to be in love with Caroline, and I know he had loved Laura when we were at uni, so why had he cheated on them? I asked him.

He had no idea either. Perhaps it was because he was pissed or horny. More likely still because he wanted the validation, or simply just because he could. He even speculated that maybe he just craved chaos, or liked having secrets. Then he floated some bullshit idea that his parents were so stable, that maybe the contrarian in him craved chaos. He'd tried to talk to his female friends about it. One of them, Erika, had told him it was because he didn't respect women enough. He wasn't sure about that, because undeniably he loved women. "Love and respect are two separate things," I told him. Either way, there was no excuse and he knew that.

At least he had recognised that he had a problem and taken some steps to address it, and I commended him on that. A period of restraint, self-control and abstinence could be just what he needed. I tried to give him some encouragement for the latent maturity he had shown. But I had the wrong end of the stick.

For a year he hadn't dated anyone, but he'd been putting his dick about more than ever. It was a miracle he hadn't caught anything. Perhaps that visit to church had helped after all. I asked him if there had been anyone he had had feelings for in that time.

There had been two. The first was a friend of Rose, the woman we saw in Gyeongju. They met on a trip to Boryeong, on Korea's West coast. They have an annual mud festival there, where people go to cover themselves in mud with supposed healing qualities and to party for the weekend. There was chemistry between them, but they never progressed beyond friends-with-benefits. Roger wasn't ready for a relationship and she didn't view him as boyfriend material. Though they never got it together, Roger sometimes wondered what could have been. The second, Christine, was one of his mates. Nothing happened between them, but he would have liked it to. Like him, she was a teacher, but she had previously been a lawyer in the US. Smart, strong and articulate, he admired her. One night they'd been talking hypotheticals at dinner and she told him she could never be with someone who lacked self-respect. She said it as banter, but Roger recognised the truth in it and it hurt.

Receiving short shrift from Christine and Erika, Roger had increasingly spent his free time with Duncan, who at that time was still dating Rose. Duncan and Roger sound like very different personalities. He described Duncan as a pretty average guy, hardly the life of the party. Regardless, the two of them clicked and whilst he was in Korea, he was Roger's best friend here. As Roger got to know Duncan better, he was impressed by his earnestness, his loyalty to Rose and the strength of his love for her. Even after she disappeared, he never gave up on their relationship, and never blamed her. Christine thought he was being naive, but something about it made an impression on Roger. Although he couldn't have put up with what Duncan did, he made Roger want to be a more devoted partner himself. Roger just wanted to make sure that he found the right person and that he could trust himself to treat her right. And in Bohyeon, he thinks he has found her.

The two of them met at Christine's leaving do last October. They flirted that night and he got her number. He stopped shagging about as soon as he met her. They met up a few times and he told her he liked her, but he wanted to build a relationship on a foundation of honesty, so he told her about his previous cheating and promiscuity. Weirdly, she seemed more bothered about his casual relationship with Rose's friend than she was about the cheating. Bohyeon didn't seem to believe that two people can be shagging without one having feelings for the other. She's probably right too. Bohyeon went a bit cold on Roger for a few weeks, but they were still messaging, and he convinced her to meet up again for a date. Understandably, she still had some reservations, but somehow, Roger managed to charm her and the two of them started dating, although not before she set some ground rules. Firstly, Roger had to stop contacting girls he had previously slept with. Secondly, if he did cheat, he had to tell her immediately. Perfectly reasonable.

Until now, Roger has managed to keep his dick in his pants, and he certainly seems to be making more of an effort with Bohyeon than he ever has with any of his previous girlfriends. She's had a hugely positive impact on him; he's stopped smoking and doesn't go out drinking as much as he used to. She gets on well with his friends and her family has been very welcoming to him. Presumably she hasn't told them about his chequered past.

As he was talking about Bohyeon, Roger seemed much happier, relieved of the guilt and self-recrimination of the last hour. He has been one of my best mates since we first met, but there was always something slightly wild and unpredictable about him. Finally, it seemed he had settled down a bit and was doing right by Bohyeon. Honestly, I felt proud of him, and privileged that I was the one he had chosen to confide all this to. But I also wanted to know what prompted this confession, and I asked him.

Roger took some time before answering before telling me that he feels that he's changed and that he wants to know what I think. I told Roger we're all changing and that neither of us is the same person we were when we met. Roger, however, felt different and said that I'm still the same guy I was. More mature, but essentially my character hasn't changed too much since uni. He on the other hand was trying to be different.

I told him he was never a bad guy. A terrible boyfriend, perhaps, but a good friend with many qualities. I said how pleased I was that he seems to have grown up a bit and finally developed a conscience (better late than never). Finally, I reminded him how lucky he is to have found someone like Bohyeon who seems to bring out the very best in him. I just hope he remembers this and doesn't fuck things up. I'm cautiously optimistic that this time he won't.

By the time we got back to the festival and met up with the girls, it was getting dark. Gangnam Style was blaring out at the main stage, and an insane-looking procession of Koreans and foreigners in fancy and traditional dress were marching, dancing, leapfrogging and gyrating about. It was all a bit of a spectacle, but at the same time too bloody noisy, so the four of us, the girls laden with shopping bags, headed back to the main town area. We had dinner and coffee, both of which were quite average, then headed back to the hotel. Claire and I are about to watch The Other Guys, which I haven't seen before, so I'll leave today's entry here.

· · ·

Thought for the day: I was looking through Claire's photos, and she got a nice one of Cheomsongdae. I'm curious about how exactly it functioned as an observatory. It's pretty tiny. Did they use telescopes? If not, why build the observatory at all if they could just see the stars outside anyway?

WEDNESDAY 3/10/2012

11.30 pm

Didn't finish watching The Other Guys. Claire and I put the vintage porno bed to good use. Pressure released.

Going to (try to) keep this quite brief. Had a long day. Got up a bit later than we had originally planned, then headed out for brunch. Baked goods at a nice bakery. Afterwards, we jumped into a taxi, heading for Hahoe (pronounced Hahwoe) Village, a lived-in Folk Village. We were going to get a bus, but Roger had cocked up the times. Mug. Anyway, we arrived at the drop-off point, bought tickets and boarded a shuttle bus, that took us up the hill to Hahoe. The village was thronging with crowds, and we headed over to a stage set in a beautiful alcove of trees on a riverbank. Shortly after we arrived, a troupe of masked dancers and traditionally dressed musicians came out and began performing.

The musicians, all men, were playing drums, horns and gongs. They were dressed in white, with a white sash tied around their foreheads. Once they were in position, they were joined on stage by the actors who wore Hahoetal, an array of well-crafted wooden masks representing different characters, from a Goddess to a butcher. Each mask had different expressions to represent their character, but the majority seemed to me to be grinning manically. They moved around on stage, acting out folk tales; including a young lady being chased by an amorous monk, a man hunting a bull, and two men arguing over a woman. Though the intricacies of the story were somewhat lost on us, it was quite a spectacle, and really heart-warming to see the traditional local culture being so well preserved, re-enacted, and enjoyed by the crowd.

The show lasted an hour and a half, after which we made a quick tour of the village. It was similar to the one Roger and I went to yesterday, but with a very important difference: people actually live here, as we found out when we tried to walk through one gate and an old lady politely yelled at us to bugger off, or words to that effect. Other buildings, were visitable such as a craftsman's workshop where the Hahoetal masks and other traditional wares, from bowls to penis totems were being carved. Roger and I managed to restrain ourselves but exchanged glances to convey our juvenile thoughts.

Back outside, one of the village's houses garden had about thirty or forty sunflowers growing in its small garden. The village was surrounded by paddy fields and other farmland, a scattering of corn husks and other crop remnants indicating they had recently been harvested. Each plot was accompanied by an attractively decorated scarecrow, some with faces similar to the masks we had seen earlier.

It was the perfect autumn setting. Despite the gorgeous weather (it was still about 22^0C), the plants were starting to yellow. Even a few of the tree leaves were just turning shades of gold, orange or red, with some littering the path that we walked upon, slowly being ground down and torn apart by the soles of hundreds of shoes. The buildings were well-kept, elegant and practical in style, and it was a welcome change from the concrete blocks of downtown Andong. There was even a church built in the traditional Korean style. The air was fresh, and best of all; I didn't notice any mosquitoes.

Sadly, we had to head off in due course, as we had to get the train back to Seoul. After getting the bus to the bottom of the hill, we found that there were no taxis. Roger looked worried and whilst Bohyeon went to check the buses, he tried to get a nearby policeman to call a taxi for us. It didn't work. The bus was already fifteen minutes late. Roger was screwing, and even Bohyeon's perma-smile disappeared. Fortunately, the bus eventually came, but even as we took our seats, Roger muttered to me that he doubted we'd be back in time for the train. We still had to pick up our bags from the hotel. The bus meandered its way up and down valleys, seeming to go in any direction but straight. Tension mounted. Finally, when we got to Andong city centre, we had just twelve minutes to grab our bags before boarding the train. The hotel was a ten-minute walk away.

Roger told the girls to go straight to the platform and he and I made our way to the bus exit, no mean feat, squeezing past at least twenty people who didn't really want to move. As soon as the doors opened, we burst out and sprinted in the direction of the hotel. I soon left Roger trailing, thinking, 'So much for all this running he has been doing.' Despite my best efforts, I could feel myself unwillingly slowing, and was beginning to fear there was no way I was going to make it, when Roger passed me, leaning out of a cab window, waving two middle fingers and yelling, "See you at the station.... jizzcock."

I couldn't help but laugh at the bastard. Not only had he made me sprint like a maniac, he'd then made me feel faintly embarrassed and topped it off with a Peep Show reference. I jogged back to the station, where the girls were just entering. They looked at me quizzically, and I explained what had happened (minus the middle fingers and the "jizzcock"). Soon, a beaming, slightly pink-faced Roger joined us at the entrance, and we headed to the platform, all of us grateful to a somewhat smug Roger, but I'll let him off this time. Joker.

The train journey was fine. As a novelty, Roger had secured us all seats, and all were near each other. The girls got some food, but Roger and I declined. It didn't look that amazing, but in fairness, what little I had of Claire's wasn't bad at all. Still, I was secretly holding out for something a bit hotter and more appetising later on. I had the image of chowing down on some Isaac's toast and was saving myself for that. I'm currently munching on some grapes and almonds, so that never really happened, but I think I'll be full enough. The grapes here are delicious; sweet and aromatic, but they don't eat the skins, instead, you squeeze out the fleshy middle and discard the skins, which are quite thick.

Anyway, where was I? I finished Adrian Mole on the train. It was excellent as ever. It took slightly over two hours to get back to Seoul, and another hour from the station, Cheonnyangni, to Roger's stop. I started on The French Lieutenant's Woman. Seems interesting so far: a retrospectively written book about the Victorian period.

Unfortunately, we had a nasty surprise waiting for us once we had parted ways with Roger and Bohyeon. Roger's flat was literally swarming with mosquitoes. They were everywhere, on the cooker, the ceiling, the bathroom mirror. Both of us were knackered, but it didn't stop us from attacking them like lunatics, myself with my bare hands, and Claire with the book that Roger had just lent her, Murakami's Underground, which was slightly ill-advised as it has a white cover.

By the end, I had amassed a total of seven of the winged cunts, and Claire had caught three and damaged the book somewhat. Not sure how she's going to explain that one. There's still a few more around. One just flew past my ear, prompting me to slap myself. Again. Actually, fuck it, that's this diary up to date anyway, I'm gonna get the little tosser. Goodnight.

Thought for the day: What is the correct plural term for a group of mosquitoes? We say 'a herd of cows', a 'flock of sheep'. I think it's a 'swarm' like with bees, but Claire thinks it's a 'cloud', but that seems more appropriate for midges. Cloud of cunts.

THURSDAY 4/10/2012

10.45 pm

I got that last mosquito last night. Red smudges marking murder scenes dot the ceiling and walls.

Today was another fairly long day. We got up around 7 as we had to head up to Seoul. Roger was taking us on a Demilitarized Zone (DMZ) trip. Unfortunately, Bohyeon hadn't been able to get the day off and had to go back to work. Roger was on top of things though and had booked us the trip and sorted the logistics. We took the tube (jihachul, Koreans call it) and changed at a station called City Hall. Unsurprisingly, this was right in the centre of central Seoul, so we were caught up in rush-hour traffic and the train was packed until we got off near Lotte Hotel. Lotte seems to be everywhere, I'd bought some Xylitol brand gum also made by Lotte and I've also seen Lotteria, a chain of burger restaurants. We found the bus, and once ensconced in its warmth, with all of his responsibilities done, Roger promptly fell asleep, missing a Q&A by a North Korean defector. Roger was sitting next to an American man and his wife, who looked Korean. The two of them seemed to be on holiday with their kids. Fortunately, the guy had the patience of a saint and just laughed whenever Roger's head lolled onto his shoulder.

The DMZ trip itself was a good insight into the tragedy of Korea's division in the aftermath of WW2. We were accompanied by a vivacious middle-aged tour guide and the North Korean defector, who answered questions as we made our way to Imjingak, the first stop on the tour. Imjingak has an old train locomotive, rusting and scarred by hundreds of bullet holes. It was left stranded during the Korean War and serves as a desolate reminder of the intensity of the fighting. Nearby is the Freedom Bridge, which was used by South Korean soldiers who were repatriated after the conflict.

Next stop was Odusan Unification Observatory, overlooking the Imjingak River and the border. You can see into North Korea and some of the houses making up the village of Kijong-dong. I couldn't see much action on that side, although I did see a car pass some of the buildings. Our guide told us that the buildings there are empty shells that long ago became uninhabitable, and had been left there for show. Post-telescoping, we were shown a rather propaganda-y video about North Korea and how a woman there had to sell her baby because of poverty.

Though the contents of the video may well be true, the presentation was so overtly politicised as 'North Korea terrible, South Korea good' that all three of us were soon weary of it, and Roger stood up in the middle and walked off. Next, we were shown around a museum exhibition of North Korean products, from souvenir pictures depicting Kim lineage as Messiah-like figures, to canned goods, wine and clothes. They had also made a mock-up of a North Korean classroom, and the defector told us about education in the schools there; how the main subjects were brainwashing propaganda and the history of Kim Il Sung and Kim Jong Il. Roger asked lots of questions that other people had already asked on the bus.

Dopey bastard. Politely though, she answered everything. Roger was quite moved by the account of her escape through China and how she had paid for her parents to come over. She had even been the target of a failed assassination.

We lunched on a beef dish called 'bulgogi' which Roger says means 'fire meat'. I was expecting it to be spicy, but it wasn't. It was cooked in front of us in a marinade, with onions and some other veg. We were served several side dishes with it too, including a cucumber kimchi and a small plate of baby crabs. After that, we were herded back on the bus and driven towards the Joint Security Area (JSA), stopping off at Camp Bonifas where an American GI boarded the bus, to act as our guide.

He then led us to a lecture hall where we had to sign a form excusing the American and Korean armies and the UN of any culpability in the case of any incidents in the DMZ. Then we watched a quick PowerPoint presentation. Well, two of us watched it; Roger fell asleep again. Something must have kept him up the night before.

From there we drove to the actual border, passing through yellowed fields around Daesong-dong, the northernmost South Korean village and the only (civilian) inhabited area within the Southern part of the DMZ. Due to its special location, there are certain conditions to living there, some being pros (e.g. exemption from conscription and taxation) and others being cons (e.g. an 11 pm curfew). I don't think I could live there. Finally, we got to the JSA and were taken through South Korea's observation building, Freedom House and onto its steps which lead right down to the buildings straddling the border itself.

Three South Korean guards stood observing the North Korean side in the 'ROK Ready' position, influenced by Taek-wondo, a position designed to both intimidate and show how ready for action the soldiers were. After the GI gave a brief lowdown on the purpose of the various different buildings and the occasional erratic behaviour of the North Korean guards, we were allowed into the central building of 'Conference Row', a row of five one-storey buildings, the outer two a metallic silver and the three in the middle were painted a light, UN-blue. Periodically, the two sides and UN representatives meet in them for discussions. I wonder if they choose one room, or have different meetings in all five. The GI didn't say.

An amusing anecdote was relayed to us where the two sides became embroiled in a battle of the flags. On consecutive days, flags of increasingly large heights were placed on the negotiation tables, to the point where they reached the ceiling. This battle of the flags can also be seen in the surrounding countryside, with towering flag poles on both sides of the border, including one on the North Korean side that was at one point the tallest flagpole in the world.

After a few posed photos with an expressionless South Korean soldier and a look around the inevitable gift shop, our bus headed back to Seoul. This time, we all fell asleep. Claire dribbled a bit on my shoulder but later denied it was her. Getting off at the Lotte hotel, Roger took us back southwards on the tube to a place called Guro. After getting out at the Jihachul station there, we had a few beers on a table outside a nearby convenience store (seemed weird, but apparently it's normal) whilst we waited for Bohyeon and some of Roger's friends to arrive before heading over to a 'Chimaek' (chicken and 'maekju' - beer) restaurant for dinner. I talked with two of his mates called Will and Adam, the former a friendly American and the latter a nice South African DJ and accountant moonlighting as a teacher here for now. Claire and Bohyeon chatted with some girls. I'm not sure why the gender divide happened, but it did. I overheard Claire asking Bohyeon what she thought about possible reunification with North Korea. Bohyeon explained the diverging opinions: how a lot of elder

Koreans want reunification, whilst the younger generations are worried about the economic implications and the fact that the North Koreans are so very different psychologically. She hadn't actually given her opinion though, so Claire asked again, and Bohyeon said she was against reunification. I was somewhat surprised, but can sort of understand her views.

After dinner, Claire and I both felt quite tired, so the four of us headed back home, whereupon we had the usual battle with mosquitoes and I killed three. Claire is already asleep in bed. It has been a long day, and I've just spent the past hour writing about it, so I think I'll join her.

Thought for the day: I think if Korea were to be reunified, whilst the first twenty years would undoubtedly be tough, long-term it would be good for the country economically. A new labour reserve would be opened up, and both sides would have to spend far less on the military and defence. Also, they might rid themselves of the occupying American forces. Perhaps the hardest part would be the integration of loyalists from the North and the clash of cultures between North and South Koreans. This would be even more pronounced than the reunification of Germany due to the Kims' cult of personality.

FRIDAY 5/10/2012

7 pm

Claire was feeling somewhat out of sorts today. I think the last week or so has taken its toll. We've both really enjoyed it, but it's been a bit hectic, and we didn't ever have much of a prolonged rest to allow us to get over the jet lag. While Claire had a long lie-in, I wrote a few postcards then checked my work emails.

At brunchtime, I went for a stroll to get us some food. The weather is still very nice, but I have to say the local area isn't the most exciting, although there are more shops and restaurants than I had realised.

I picked us up some pots of ramen, as everyone always seems to go on about it. Also grabbed two kimbaps (like long sticks of the sushi where stuff is rolled in seaweed) from one of the local restaurants. Roger told me lots of people get them as takeout, and they're pretty good. Upon my return, we lunched and then spent the rest of the afternoon watching movies, snuggling, and well, the stuff that couples invariably do after a lot of snuggling. Enough said.

Being at home today with my darling Claire, I felt obliged to defend her against the Mosquito Luftwaffe. Ended up killing four throughout the day, including two one-handed catches right out of the air. I could tell that Claire was secretly a little bit proud of me. Roger called us at 5 and suggested he come round at 7.30 for dinner and to head out for some drinks with his friends around here. After a day indoors, it sounds ideal. Unfortunately, Bohyeon won't be joining us as she's got some work to do for tomorrow. Anyway, that's all for today.

(Saturday) 11 am

Roger cooked us Indian food before we went out last night. Well, he said it was Indian food, but it wasn't like the Indian food that we might find in our tandoori restaurants back home. He calls that stuff 'schlop', and says it's engineered for the British palette. I've heard all this before, so it was a familiar rant. I suppose he'd know having travelled in India quite extensively. His food was nice, but I'm not sure if I liked it as much as the schlop, and had an odd yearning for Spice Garden around the corner from our place.

After dinner, Roger and I tried to figure out how the mosquitoes are getting into the apartment. He killed three and I killed two, and I have to say his cat-like reflexes impressed me. He's a good ally in the War on Mozzies. Our best guess at the minute is through the air conditioning unit or the bathroom vent.

Once our dinner had settled, we taxied to Sanbon, the area we came to on our first evening here. First was Pirate Bar, a place where beer is served in plastic cups placed in sleeves of ice, all held together with a plastic retainer of sorts (luckily including a handle). When the drink is finished, the ice sleeve is removed and thrown at a target, which if hit, gives the thrower a chance of winning a free drink. We drank three beers there, and despite Roger and my best efforts, including a cricket bowl and a baseball pitch from Roger, it was Claire who finally hit the target, winning herself a tequila. She hates tequila, but fortunately, Roger doesn't.

Roger, unsurprisingly was in his element in the local bars and seemed to know almost all of the foreigners and a fair few of the Koreans present. Before we left Pirate Bar, we were joined by two of his friends, Keith and James. Roger told us Keith is somewhat of a Lothario. He's an American artist teaching in Korea in the latest leg of what seems to be a life-long world tour. I have no idea of his actual prowess with the fairer sex, but he's certainly a country slut, having been to over sixty countries. Keith was accompanied by Josie, a (ex?) girl-friend, visiting from America, who Claire latched onto at the first whiff of a double-X chromosome. Why do girls always do that?

Anyway, the gender lines were drawn and stayed as such until James' girlfriend, Juhui (who some people were calling Julie), came along shortly after we reached the next bar. James and Juhui are an odd couple. James, a giant of a man, is a laid-back Canadian who speaks little Korean. Juhui is a petite Korean nurse who speaks little English and is as intense and frankly off the wall as James is easy-going. Somehow though, they seem to complement one another, certainly more than Keith and his lady friend.

The bar, called 'My Friends' was a 'Bottle Bar' where we could help ourselves from the fridge. At Pirate Bar, we'd been drinking Cass, a dreadful, synthetic-tasting lager, so I moved on to some European beer as we played a few games of darts. Darts in Korea is a bit different to back home, with plastic darts thrown at perforated boards in place of metal darts being thrown at corkboards. I was sceptical at first, but in fairness, it was quite fun, with a built-in computer to calculate the points, and a variety of games. One such game sees you somehow 'invading Japan' by throwing darts at the board. It made absolutely no sense to me.

Roger wanted to stay out longer, but Claire and I were beyond tipsy. We headed home without him around 2 am, and after a little bit more snuggling (thanks beer), the two of us went to sleep.

Thought for the day: Korean food: great. Korean beer: less great.

SATURDAY 6/10/2012

11.40 am

I have a sneaking suspicion that Roger had a very late one, as we'd heard nothing of him all morning until a few minutes ago when he told us to be ready in half an hour to go out for what he calls breakfast. The two of us had been up for the past hour and a half, and eaten some cereal and a banana already. I put a wash on and cleaned Roger's flat whilst Claire got ready. I put the hoover to excellent use and managed to suck up three more mosquitoes using the nozzle, one from the ceiling and two from the window.

Our washing machine at home was playing up before we left and I have no idea if the landlord has fixed it, but at least this way we'll have some clean clothes for when we get back. Anyway, guess I better go and get properly dressed myself. Over and out.

(Sunday) 9 am

Claire's still asleep. Bit wary for when she wakes up actually. She was quite pissed off with Roger and me last night, and for my part, I'm very disappointed with Roger. It was a very messy evening, but I'll get to that in due course.

When Roger appeared at our door just after midday, he confirmed my suspicions by looking absolutely horrendous and having a vague smell of alcohol about him, even though he'd tried to cover it by showering and overdosing on the after-shave. His eyes were a painful red, with deep, dark, sagging bags beneath them. I was quite amused, but Claire was less than impressed.

After lunch, we headed up to town, disembarking at a station close to a small park and a stream which leads into the much bigger river Han that runs through Seoul. People were positioning picnic blankets and small tents for the Seoul Fireworks Festival, which wasn't due to start for another few hours. Parents tried to keep their impatient children entertained, whilst beside them, circles of elderly men or women chatted, raising noisy toasts of soju to whatever they were toasting. Couples, protective of their privacy, sat slightly separated from these noisier revellers, in niches set between small trees, or right down by the bank of the Han.

SLRs were in abundance, and Claire gave us a run down of who had the best cameras and why people needed tripods for fireworks. It was interesting enough for me, and a pleasure as ever to hear her speak passionately about something, but Roger was in no fit state to participate in the conversation. He walked several steps in front of us, distracting me from my photography lesson as we observed him stumbling in diago-nals, tacking like a bearded, human yacht, albeit with none of the grace or splendour.

We walked along the Han for a good while. Crossing it on the subway had given me no real idea of quite how wide it is. It was nice enough, but not quite as scenic as the Thames. Few iconic buildings lined its shores, at least on the stretch we passed along. Compare that to London with the Houses of

Parliament, St Paul's, MI6, the Tate Modern and the Dome. It felt like something was missing, and both Claire and Roger agreed with me that it didn't have quite the same charm.

After a while, Roger led us to a station called Noksapyeong, fed by two railway lines beneath a multi-levelled cylindrical style station lined with shops and cafés. Claire remarked how it would make a cool location for a photo shoot. From there we walked to a nearby restaurant called 'Petra Palace', where we were to meet some more of Roger's friends for dinner.

They arrived in dribs and drabs, first a cheery Blackburner, Tim and a mixed-race Korean-white American called Annie. The food at the restaurant was good, and Claire and I both enjoyed a nice shish kebab, chicken for her, mutton for me. Roger's friends too, seemed nice, and at our next destination, a bar called Dillinger's, we were joined by two more of Roger's friends, a Korean woman about our age called Eunjyu and an old school friend of Roger's, Japinder, who I had met once before in England at one of Roger's birthday parties.

It was at Dillinger's that the night started to get slightly messy. By slightly, what I actually mean is terribly messy. Japinder, Tim, Roger and I played (actual, non-plastic) darts whilst the ladies bonded. Japinder and Tim were both darts sharks ("darks" as Japinder put it), and Roger and I sat down after being comprehensively beaten in the first game. The girls were talking about fashion, and Roger launched into it with gusto. This didn't seem like the Roger that I knew, and soon enough I saw what he was doing, as he twisted the topic to get the girls talking about one another's clothes.

It's a skill he's always had. He enters into a conversation, thinking several steps ahead and manipulating it to his advantage. I had no idea how he was going to manipulate it, but having been familiar with Roger and his exploits (particularly concerning women) for almost a decade, I should have guessed. It wasn't until he complimented Eunjyu on her skirt (both tight and short) with his eyes twinkling that I saw what he was up to, and I gave him a look which I hoped would say, 'What exactly are you doing here mate?' Still, he gave me a wink and returned his attention to Eunjyu. I ignored it, reasoning a bit of flirting is harmless enough.

We had a few drinks at Dillinger's. Roger suggested we go over to a club in Hongdae. I was up for it and so were Tim and Japinder. Claire, however, was tired and didn't want to go, and said we were going home. Roger and I conspired to persuade her to go out anyway. We ordered one more round, splitting the bill between us. When we sat down, Claire wagged her finger at us and said, "Right, we're going home after this drink. I'm not asking you, I'm telling you." I'm accustomed to Claire being at the end of her tether and knew the consequences if we didn't go home, but Roger was clearly a bit offended by this behaviour, and looking her coolly in the eyes said, "My dear Claire, you are not anyone's boss here, well except maybe his," and gave a cheeky nod in my direction.

Slightly embarrassed by Roger's remark, and eager to prove that I wasn't entirely whipped, I resolved that I too was staying out. Claire picked up her coat and bag and looking at me said, "Right, we're going home."

"I don't know how to get back," I said, a half-truth.

She glared at me, then turned towards Roger and said, "How do we get back?"

"If you'd asked me with a please or some other common courtesy, I might have told you, but there's no way I'm going to now. We're going to Hongdae."

I smiled at this and got treated to Claire's finest dragon eyes in return. Annie and Eunjyu soon stepped in and attempted to extinguish the fire in her eyes, even talking Hongdae up to the point where I think Claire was secretly looking forward to it. It's hard to say because she was so sequestered away with those ladies, barely even casting me a cursory glare. This continued on the way down to the subway, and when I tried to take her hand, she didn't return my grasp, and soon slipped her hand away. It wasn't until I offered her the last open seat on the train that she uttered an icy, "Thanks."

She seemed to have perked up somewhat by the time we got to Hongdae. Claire had always loved clubbing when we first started going out, but we hadn't been for a while, and I think the prospect of having a dance and some cocktails excited her a bit.

Once out of the station, Roger took us to a park evidently used as a large gathering space for the local university youth as well as those in the area for a night out. There, he bought us two bottles of something called 'makgoli', a creamy-looking drink which Tim termed "Alcoholic Korean jizz," although I believe it's actually a form of rice 'wine'. The guy he bought it off was a weathered middle-aged man who exhibited the broadest smile I've ever seen in my life. Roger assured me that everyone knows him as 'Makgoli Man' and that he is some-what of a Hongdae celebrity. We all had a cup (or in Roger's case several cups) of makgoli outside a small 'bar' of sorts which seemed to be run out of a garage. The girls were talking to some male friends of Eunjyu and one of them tried to chat up Claire, but she made it abundantly clear that she was uninterested and even pointed me out to the guy. I had to smile inside. However annoyed she gets, she never tries to make me jealous or anything. One of the many reasons I love her.

Tim led us over to a restaurant where we were supposed to pick up his friends before going to a bar, but we ended up staying there for ages. The restaurant was one of these 'gourmet burger' bars, but we'd eaten, and I have no real idea why we stayed there. One beer got ordered, then another, then another. It was a bit of a disappointment to be honest, as I was hoping to go to a bar or club. Claire was ensconced in her bevy of ladies, and very obviously giving me the cold shoulder to the point of not even asking me when we were leaving.

Eventually, I began to tire too and turned to Roger to ask him when we were leaving, but he wasn't there. I'd been so engrossed talking with Tim and Japinder about the football that I had failed to notice this absence. Also, I'd been ignoring my bladder so decided to go and empty that before looking for him.

The bathroom was through a large black door at the side of the restaurant, beside a set of stairs. My bladder emptied, and a stray mosquito killed, I walked out of the bathroom but was stopped in my tracks by the faintest, "Shhhhhh". There was a pause and the sort of silence when two people are consciously trying to avoid being overheard. I pushed the door back to the restaurant and stomped my feet, but stayed exactly where I was. My suspicions were already aroused.

A few seconds later, a female voice whispered, "Have they gone?" followed by a male voice murmuring something even quieter, slightly muffled. I couldn't work out what had been said, but I knew it was Roger. Seconds later, I heard the distinct sounds of lips meeting and clothes rustling. Tiptoeing over to the stairs, I looked up and saw Roger kissing Eunjyu, his left hand against the wall, and his right hand up Eunjyu's skirt. She had her tights pulled down to her knees and her right hand in the vicinity of Roger's crotch. I stood there, speechless. I couldn't understand Roger at all. Bohyeon was the better-looking of the two women for a start, but more than that, she was intelligent, understanding and kind. Eunjyu on the other hand, seemed somewhat shallow and self-obsessed.

I continued to watch them, the two of them oddly trans-fixing. Eunjyu must have sensed my presence, and it was she who broke off kissing Roger, and looked straight down at me.

Roger must have assumed this was her coming up for air, and he proceeded to smother her neck with kisses until she tugged his hand out from within her skirt. Finally, Roger looked down at me, and as our eyes met, his jaw fell. It was almost exactly like what had happened back in Leeds with Jessie when I'd caught them in the stairwell of Creation.

At first, I wasn't so much angry as sad and disappointed. Just like Laura and Caroline and the others Roger had cheated on, Bohyeon was going to be the one to suffer now, and just like back in Leeds, I was the poor sap stuck in the middle of it all. More than anything though, I saw Roger for what he really is. Although he can be a great bloke, he's just a selfish, impulsive tosser, who has to be the most romantically reckless person I know. He still doesn't seem to have fully realised that there are consequences to his actions and that he hurts other people and above all himself. My stare must have said everything I just related because Roger recoiled as if wounded. I flashed one last glare at them then walked out. By then I was angry.

Gonna have to end this here for now as Claire is stirring. Going to make her a cup of tea, then close this down. I haven't decided what to tell her yet, and I think she's probably going to be a bit pissed off with me too.

(Sunday) 11.30 am

Claire's in the shower. Bohyeon just called me. We're meeting for lunch at Paris Baguette across the road in an hour. Back to last night...

Heading back into the restaurant, I walked straight up to Claire.

"Sorry hon, you must be tired. Do you wanna go soon?"

She probably knew something was up; I never call her 'hon'.

"Erm, OK, I thought you wanted to go to the club?" she said cooly.

"I feel bad making you stay out," I said, with only a hint of truth. There was a bit of guilt, although that wasn't why I wanted to leave.

"OK, let me finish my drink first." She then proceeded to rush her cocktail. I did the same, downing the half glass of beer I had left.

Just as I was finishing my pint, Roger came out, staring at the floor, but that couldn't hide how flushed he was. I glared at him, told him we were going home and asked if he was coming. He paused for a while and cast a look back to the stairwell door. "OK," he said. We said our goodbyes to everyone, Roger's friends beseeching him to stay out, and the girls giving Claire the kind of hugs they'd give to lifelong friends they hadn't seen in years. I shook hands with everyone but managed to avoid Eunjyu's, who had hung back from the rest of the group. I had some idea where her hand had been. She looked sheepishly at me as I glared at her and said, "Goodbye," very coldly. I wished I hadn't asked Roger if he was coming—I guess I thought I could spare him doing any more harm— because I'd rather he hadn't.

We walked briskly to the main road and seeing a line of taxis, I flagged one down. Roger was hanging back slightly and Claire had ignored my outstretched hand. It was going to be an awkward ride home. We drove back in complete silence. Claire soon fell asleep. Roger sat in the front, but I had nothing to say to him. Well, I had one thing, and I said it. I caught him looking at me in the windshield mirror and I said, "Don't look at me, you're an idiot." He took my advice.

We pulled up near Roger's flat. I gently woke Claire up, and Roger got out. He paid for the taxi, and even though I should have given him at least half, I was so pissed off with him that I just let him. As Claire and I got out, Roger made to walk off in the direction of Bohyeon's. I had failed to notice until this point that Claire was quite tipsy, the alcohol having caught up with her. She called out to Roger, her voice shrill with alcohol and tiredness.

"You're not going to say goodnight Rogeee?"

"Oh sorry Claire, I thought you were still asleep," he said, after turning around. He walked towards us and sheepishly hugged Claire. I glared at him.

He then went to hug me, but I made no move to reciprocate, so instead he offered his hand.

"Night mate," he said. I stepped back from his hand, wondering if he'd washed it and then stared him dead in the eyes. He glanced at Claire, and I turned to her. She was swaying, looking at us. She might have been tipsy, but she knew something was up. Reluctantly, I shook Roger's hand, glaring angrily at him as I did.

"Goodnight," I said.

Claire and I walked back to the apartment in silence. It wasn't until we were back in the room that she asked me if something had happened. I said it was nothing. She pressed me on it, and I said that I had told him that I wanted to go home earlier. It was already 4 am. She half-bought it, and I got myself off the hook in that respect, but I'm sure she still thinks something's up. In bed, I put my arm around her, but she shrugged it off, and moved further across the bed, taking the sheets with her. I turned my back on her. Thoughts swirled in my head, and I couldn't sleep. I didn't get to sleep until after 5. At 6.30 I woke up, needing the toilet. Claire had pulled back next to me, her arm lying loosely on my chest.

Thought for the day: Do people ever really change, and if they do, how much of it is superficial or temporary? Is there a tendency to revert to type, however hard they try not to?

SUNDAY 7/10/2012

12.05 pm

Usually, I find writing my journal cathartic, but having written up last night, if anything, I feel more pissed off.

When we got up, I got a ticking off from Claire. Rightly so to be fair. I think she was more annoyed with Roger but she's not one to hold a grudge, although, she might if she'd seen what I'd seen. Like me, she just wants to enjoy our last day in Korea, so we hugged it out, and things are fine now.

She had only the vaguest recollection of some tension between Roger and me last night, and when she asked what happened, I said that it was just drunken bickering. She asked about what, and I said it was just "lads' banter" that got a bit out of control. She raised eyebrows at that, but said, "OK". That's another reason I'm annoyed with Roger, because of him, I've lied to Claire. She's doing her hair and makeup at the minute, so there's no way she can see this, and ever since she saw the comment about Bohyeon in Gyeongju, I've been a lot more careful about leaving the file open.

She's a bit hungover from last night, and though she won't admit it, I think she actually had a good time. The girls seemed pretty nice, and she was enthusing about them all, even

Eunjyu. Luckily I don't think she saw my face when she mentioned her, as I'm sure it was momentarily thunderous. I know that Roger's the one responsible for his actions, but the mention of Eunjyu's name gave me an instant flashback. I'm going to have to control my emotions a bit today so that Bohyeon and Claire don't catch on. At some point, I'll have to speak to Roger about all of this. I had an inclination to go straight to Bohyeon and tell her, but Roger's one of my best mates and he's been a good host to us. What's more, this is his mess, and his to sort out. I really don't want to become more embroiled in it all.

Anyway, Claire's almost ready, and I'm just about up to date on all of this. I've been typing since I woke up at 9 am, and only had a banana and two cups of tea, so I'm starving right now. Today is our last day in Korea, and though it has been soured by last night, we've had a great trip. I just want to get through the day without Claire and Bohyeon finding out what happened. No need for a shadow to be cast over their memories of our visit, so I want them to enjoy our last day as much as possible.

8.30 pm

Claire's doing the packing at the minute. She likes everything just so, and having insisted that I'm useless at packing, has taken over from me. I have to say I'm nowhere near as untidy or disorganised as she makes out sometimes, although she does have very high standards in those respects. Still, I can't complain as it gives me the chance to crack on with this.

Lunch was a standard affair at Paris Baguette. I had some sort of Danish pastry with sausage and cheese instead of apples. The bread was a bit sweet, but pretty nice anyway. I looked about for baguettes but saw none. False advertising. Claire and Roger were visibly hung-over and though I mostly felt OK, I was a bit dehydrated and my brain was intermittently throbbing. Nobody was talking much, only Bohyeon breaking the silence with questions about the DMZ tour or the last two days. At first, these were mostly directed at Claire but met by grunts and insightful sentences including, "It was really nice," subsequent questions were directed to me, and I was happy to elaborate on Claire's answers.

Sensing the mood (i.e. hungover), Bohyeon bought us each a bottle of water before we headed to the station, giving us strict instructions to drink as much as we could before we got there. Roger also produced a packet of paracetamol which he shared out among us. Whilst taking the paracetamol, I took a swig of water, not looking at the floor, and tripped on a piece of uneven pavement. I almost completely stacked it and sent the water rushing down the wrong hole, choking myself. The others thought this was a lot funnier than I did. In fairness, I should have known by now to look where I'm going. I have noticed that Korea goes for aesthetics over practicality when it comes to paved areas. Most pavements in Gunpo are lined with yellow, green, blue and red tiles or slabs, and other parts are strange, spongy green or red tarmacked areas. These look nice enough, but aren't always even, meaning more care is required than I demonstrated.

Anyway, after twenty minutes or so, my headache was gone, and by the time we got up to Seoul, Claire and Roger had perked up slightly. With his hangover subsiding, Roger seemed to be trying a bit too hard, as if to be the perfect host and boyfriend. As we strolled along a pretty landscaped stream called Cheongyechon, him holding hands with Bohyeon, I couldn't help but think about where that hand had been the night before.

I hadn't really noticed it before, but Seoul is definitely a city for couples, and Cheongyecheon was packed with them, young and old, from high schoolers to grandparents, with a clutch of parents trying to keep their children from falling into the water. The stream, below street level, is accessed by sets of stairs and runs through one of the main areas of Seoul. It's somewhat of an oddity, a place of tranquillity amidst the concrete jungle. In Seoul, it seems that most people are in a rush, but by Cheongyecheon, people take their time, strolling along, taking in the atmosphere, stopping to sit under a bridge and watch the water flow by. It's something special.

The stream ends (or begins really) with an illuminated artificial waterfall where we stopped for some photos. Bohyeon took a photo of me and Claire which came out quite nicely, after which Bohyeon and Roger were messing about doing all sorts of silly poses. Claire then said, "OK, one of the boys." Reluctantly, I went and stood with Roger. He put his arm around me, but I just crossed my arms. Claire took another and told me to look less serious. Though I was trying to act natural around Roger, the way he was acting was pissing me off, as if nothing had happened and everything was fine. I tried to force a smile for the next photo, but it didn't convince.

"You look like a serial killer," Claire said when she showed me the photo.

We exited Cheongyechon onto Sejong-ro. This area, Gwanghwamun, has been lent its name by an important gate to the royal palace and is perhaps better known to tourists for its two famous statues. Roger started to tell us about them, but I cut him off and said, "How about letting Bohyeon, the actual Korean tell us about them?" He seemed a bit hurt and Claire gave me a look, but I was sick of the sound of his voice. Bohyeon didn't seem to mind and took on the role of tour guide.

The first statue was of Yi Sun-Shin, who holds a similar role in Korea's national legend to our own Horatio Nelson for his efforts in repeatedly repelling and sabotaging the Japanese forces. He foiled Japan's invasions of Korea and China by destroying much of their fleet, and with it, their supply routes, leading to Japanese retreats from Korea, which had already been largely conquered on land. At the Battle of Myeongnyang in 1597, he used a narrow strait and misty conditions to trap and defeat a fleet of one hundred and thirty-three Japanese ships with just thirteen of his own, losing not a single ship. Pretty phenomenal.

Not far behind the statue of Yi Sun Sin is a statue of another of the greatest Koreans, King Sejong. Sejong ruled in the fifteenth century, overseeing a golden age in Korea and he's also credited with creating the Korean alphabet. This saw a huge increase in literacy amongst the common people. Bohyeon told me that the alphabet is very phonetic and Roger chimed in that he was able to pick it up after just a few hours of study. I wish that I'd put in the effort myself, even if it was just for nine days. It would be cool to be able to read Korean, although I'd have no idea of the meaning of the words.

Next, we headed over to Gwanghwamun itself, the gate leading to the royal palace, Gyeongbukgung. The palace is more a complex of palatial buildings. Much of it was destroyed by fire and later rebuilt, only for the Japanese to destroy most of it during their colonisation of Korea. In recent years it has been restored and rebuilt to make it as close to the original style as possible. Though I suspect it may be a slightly simplified and sanitised version of the original, I have to say I was really impressed with the level of detail and the touches which made the complex look authentic. This and Bulguksa, have really made me respect how South Korea has tried to rebuild its past. Having lost so much during the Japanese occupation and the Korean War that followed, they clearly realise the significance of their national history and why it must be preserved.

It was also in Gyeongbukgung that I was finally able to speak with Roger. I waited until Bohyeon and Claire got deeply engrossed in a conversation, then asked Roger a fairly innocuous question (it was a classic, "What do you think this was for?" whilst pointing at a large black cauldron) and then indicated to him to hang back. I then led him off in a different direction to the girls. We walked for a few minutes in silence, as I wanted to make sure there was no chance that the girls had followed. It wasn't until we were in a small courtyard of one of the less-important buildings that I looked him in the eye and said, "You're a fucking idiot." Eloquent, I know.

He agreed without hesitation. It was nothing like the confrontation we'd had all those years before where we'd nearly come to blows when I called him out for cheating on Laura. At least he's grown up in some respects since then and can take responsibility for his actions now. Sort of.

I asked him what the hell he was thinking, but he didn't answer, instead telling me that however angry I was, he was more annoyed with himself than I could possibly be. I wasn't going to let him off that easily. After all that shit he talked about the other day about wanting to be a better, more devoted person, less than one week later and he had cheated on his girlfriend. So what had happened in between?

When Roger had come over and cooked dinner on Friday night, he'd just had a big fight with Bohyeon. He hadn't let on at all, of course, but then he's a master of deception. Bohyeon had asked him not to go out that night, and he'd responded that she was being controlling. This then escalated, bringing a series of prior arguments and lingering grievances back to the surface, culminating in Roger walking out and over to see us. Whilst we were out in Sanbon, Eunjyu had messaged him and said that she missed him. He was drunk and pissed off with Bohyeon, so ended up inviting Eunjyu to come out on Saturday. I asked him if he had done this before, and he admitted he'd messaged her once or twice when he and Bohyeon had previously argued, but they had never actually met up. Next, I asked him who he wanted to be with: Eunjyu or Bohyeon. He replied, "Bohyeon, unequivocally," but then admitted that there is, or was something between him and Eunjyu.

That's when I realised that Eunjyu was the friend of Rose's that he had talked about when we were in Andong. I asked Roger if my guess was right and he confirmed it. Nothing had ever developed between them, they hadn't dated or shared their feelings, but for some time, they sought one another out whenever one of them had the urge. They'd never put a label on it, and though Roger had thought there might be the possibility of something deeper, she was inscrutable and never gave him the suggestion that she wanted anything deeper. He even speculated that he was her bit of rough, the 'exotic foreigner' she called when she was horny or wanted a self-esteem boost. I called bullshit and told him he wasn't exotic, but he said that here, he is. We were getting off-topic, so I challenged why he had even messaged her back, in spite of his supposed love for Bohyeon and the rules she had set him.

Roger didn't know. He said that whenever he argues with Bohyeon, he gets this irrational fear, knowing that she's too good for him. He's just waiting until she realises that, or until he fucks things up and she leaves. It seems this is becoming a self-fulfilling prophecy as his unfaithfulness only goes to prove that he's right.

I told him that every couple argues and that didn't mean that she was going to leave him. He said that he knows that, but whenever he's drunk, he doesn't act rationally. His old impulses hit in and he flirts with women. He speculated that perhaps he's just keeping his options open for when things inevitably go wrong with Bohyeon, but I felt he was just making excuses for himself and deflecting away from another issue, namely his drinking and I told him so.

As I suspected, most of the arguments he has with Bohyeon are when he's drunk, and similarly the times he feels most insecure about the relationship are also when he's drunk. Correlation doesn't always mean causation, but in this case, the evidence seems damning. What was perhaps most infuriating for me was that this was just history repeating itself. Roger gets drunk, then acts as if this gives himself an excuse to shed his inhibitions and act on his instincts, however immoral and irrational they are. It was almost exactly what happened with Laura at university, and not dissimilar to what he told me had happened with Caroline. Then, after all that talk, the supposed new-found responsibility, maturity and faithfulness, he does it again. Every single time he gets something, someone good, he throws it all away, hurts that person and hurts himself. It was so tiring watching him fuck things up for himself over and over again, with good, undeserving people hurt even more in the process.

I told Roger all of this and for a while he was silent. We walked on, past a large pond with a pavilion in the middle. Roger seemed to be thinking about what he wanted to say, but when he did finally speak, it didn't make sense. He said that he had invited me here because I was his best friend and he wanted to show me that he had changed and finally grown up. I just lost it when he said that. I turned to him and spoke more angrily and aggressively than I knew I could.

How could he possibly say that he had changed? Here we were, eight years after I had caught Roger cheating on Laura, and Roger was still sabotaging his own happiness, betraying somebody he supposedly loved. Nothing had changed, he hadn't grown up, and once again, I was the one who was caught in the middle. I told him this was the second time now and if it ever happens again, we were done. Roger said he got it and apologised again, but I told him if he's going to apologise, it needs to be to Bohyeon. He squirmed and looked away from me and I said to him, "You are going to tell her, right?" he dragged his hand through his hair and seemed to be unsure before finally asking me if I would tell her. I told him that this was his mess, so he had to tell her. His eyes were almost pleading as he said, "If I do, she'll leave me," but he was looking for sympathy in the wrong place. I told him he needs to stop drinking as well, to which he attempted his roguish charm and said that he's more fun when he's drinking, but I shut him straight down: he wasn't last night.

We walked on in silence, looping around the lake and pavilion and heading back towards where we left the girls. I could see a bathroom ahead of us and we both headed in. I washed my hands and splashed my face, and Roger copied me. When we walked out, water clung to his beard, twinkling as it caught the sun. He still hadn't answered whether he would tell her, so I asked him once again and he said he would, it's the right thing to do, although he'd wait until we had left. I felt relieved, partly that a sense of duty wouldn't force me to do it, but also because I could see my friend's remorse. He wasn't a complete arsehole. I extended my hand to him, satisfied it was finally clean. Roger asked me, "Friends again?" and I pulled him in for a hug. I love the guy, but I wish he'd stop hurting himself and others.

After hugging it out, Roger called Bohyeon to find out where they were. We ended up finding them at a circle of stone carvings depicting the Chinese Zodiac. When we met up with them, Roger gave Bohyeon a big hug and picked her up. She giggled with laughter and kissed him on the forehead.

"Are you two good now?" Claire asked me whilst they played about.

"Yeah, we're good," I said.

At the circle, all of us posed by the stone statue relevant to us. I found out that I am a Wood Rat, as is Roger. Claire is a Wood Ox, and Bohyeon a Fire Tiger. I can't deny that I felt an odd, misplaced sense of jealousy that Bohyeon is a Fire Tiger. That sounds so much cooler than a Wood Rat. We then strolled around the pagoda nearby, which has to rank among the most impressive buildings I've seen in Korea. Claire thought so too, and was taking photos from every angle imaginable.

From Gyeongbukgung we walked over to Insadong, an important cultural area. The main high street in Insadong is pedestrianised, much like in Myeongdong. However, unlike in Myeongdong, where the area has been given over completely to capitalism and Western brand names are proudly displayed everywhere you look, Insadong has a far more civilised and unique style. Many of the shops are privately owned craft shops, selling everything from local pottery and china to furniture and souvenirs. Even the big brand names, be they American or Korean, had their names written in the Korean alphabet, which was a nice touch. It's a shame that's not more consistent throughout Korea really. By this time we were starting to get a bit peckish again, so Roger led us down a small offshoot road to somewhere where we could get a quick, but good meal. Claire ordered a type of bibimbap, whilst I went for bulgogi, which wasn't all that much like the one we had at the DMZ, but was if anything better.

We continued walking through Insadong, which took an inordinately long time. Claire was taking lots of photos, and both girls would rush over to look at random cute or shiny things now and then. Roger took me over to a stall where they were making local sweets using honey and flour, accompanied by a strange song. They somehow manipulated the ingredients into thousands of strings, which were then wrapped around a dollop of nutty paste, to make several large sweets. I noticed Roger kept calling the sweets 'candy' and accused him of becoming Americanised. He looked hurt.

Once finally through Insadong, we took the subway home, stopping briefly at a supermarket for soju and noodles etc. for the guys back home, oh, and at Baskin Robbins for ice cream. Claire's almost finished packing and I'm downloading a movie. Bohyeon and Roger are gonna come over and watch it with us, and I dare say we'll have a few beers to go with it. Not particularly looking forward to going home, or to the long flight tomorrow. One thing I am looking forward to is being far away from all these bloody mosquitoes. I've killed four this evening already. I'm about to tidy up and wipe the murder scenes from the walls and ceiling of Roger's flat.

(Monday) 10.35 am

The four of us watched the Japanese film Rinne (meaning reincarnation). Quite dark, pretty spooky. We sat about talking for a while after the film had finished, Roger and I sharing embarrassing stories about one another to our girl-friends, but really it was for our own indulgence. Roger also mentioned that his friend, Duncan, had bought a plane ticket to Seoul. It was a fun final evening, but eventually, tiredness caught up with us all. After Roger and Bohyeon went home, Claire and I went to bed, later than we should have and with that weird, twitchy feeling you have after watching a horror film.

Thought for the day: Had somewhat of a moral dilemma today. Part of me thought I should be honest and tell Bohyeon or Claire what I'd seen. The other part told me that it wasn't my business and that I shouldn't get involved. Eventually, though, I said what I said to Roger, and I'll stick to that. I have to have faith in him that he'll (try to) do what's best. He and Bohyeon are a good couple. I hope he doesn't sabotage himself again.

MONDAY 8/10/2012

10.45 am

We'll be boarding the plane soon. I got up at 6.30 am. Made us some tea, had a shower, and exterminated two mozzies whilst doing so. Smashed one against the shower ceiling, and for the other one, used the shower to wash it off the mirror and down the sink. I can only presume it drowned. Roger and Bohyeon came to meet us at 7.30, and we bade a fond goodbye to Bohyeon. She's been a great host to us, organised a lot of our trip, and has been a very good companion to Claire. She's a lovely girl, and I hope Roger treats her right from now on.

Roger helped us get a taxi to the airport bus stop in Sanbon and we got a bus at 8.20. He has also been a fantastic host, and Saturday night aside, great company. We're both very grateful to him. Just before we got on the bus, as I hugged him goodbye, I whispered into his ear, "Don't fuck things up."

"I won't. Thanks for coming to see me, man," he said.

The bus journey was pretty unremarkable. Claire again insisted on having the window seat and again fell asleep. A solitary mosquito was flitting against the window just above her head, so I leant over and gave it the gentlest of high fives so as not to wake her. Probably the last of the little buggers I'll kill here.

I felt sad as we drove towards the airport, and I felt bad for Roger too. He always seems to be set on self-destruction. We've had a brilliant holiday. It's an interesting country and seems to be moving forward, unlike the beloved country we're set to return to, which is at best standing still. Even the airport here is better.

Anyway, I'm sitting here drinking a coffee whilst Claire is looking around the Duty-Free shops. We checked in, got our boarding passes, and passed through security. All that remains is a final thought for the day, but I can't really think of one for now, so I'll leave it for later.

5.40 pm *(written on board the plane)*

Thought for the ~~day~~ trip: I just skimmed through everything I've written whilst on this trip, and I have to say I was far more verbose than I usually am with my diaries. This is perhaps most telling when you look at how much I went on about the mosquitoes that laid mine and Claire's bodies under siege, only to suffer my wrath in return. Anyway, odd little statistic; the number of mosquitoes I personally killed (well, that I recorded killing anyway) stands at exactly fifty. If we include the nine full days we stayed here, plus the two 'half days'- i.e. when we arrived and when we left as one day, that means fifty mosquitoes in roughly ten days. Five mosquitoes a day. Somewhat impressive. That'll teach the little pricks.

REVIEWS

Enjoyed this book? Didn't?

Either way, please consider leaving a review or rating on Amazon or your preferred platform.

Honest reviews give independent authors the best opportunity to get the attention of other readers.

For more stories, please sign up to the author's newsletter at: www.dlward.co.uk

ACKNOWLEDGMENTS

Most importantly, I thank my incredible wife, Mina, and my Mum for their unwavering support and patience.

Thanks to Laura, Kathleen and Chryso for their feedback and notes. Special thanks to Steve Carey-Walton for his detailed and patient input on three separate drafts of this novella. His book, Where the Butterflies Sleep, is unlike anything you've ever read. Highly recommended.

Thanks to Dan Dunahee. Your support and appreciation of Eight Seasons helped urge me on to finish this.

Finally, thanks to Iva, one of my best mates, who visited me in South Korea.

ABOUT THE AUTHOR

D.L. Ward is a term-time teacher and a holiday author from London currently living and working in Sydney. From 2009-2013, he taught English in South Korea, where he fell in love with teaching and writing. Upon returning to London, he met his future partner, briefly worked in a rather strange office job and then trained as a Humanities teacher at an even stranger school.

D.L. Ward released his first novel, Eight Seasons in 2024. The story ties into events mentioned in the story you have just read and revolves around Roger's friend, Duncan and his girlfriend, Rose. To find out more about D.L. and what he's working on, visit www.dlward.co.uk and sign up to the mailing list.

ALSO BY D.L. WARD

EIGHT SEASONS

South Korea, 2009. Mid-twenties Londoner, Duncan Greenway lands at Incheon Airport, fleeing betrayal and seeking a new life as an English teacher. A fateful encounter with a beautiful, independent and intriguing local, Rose, soon helps Duncan to put his past behind him. Rose, however, is less able to escape her past and very soon, it begins to engulf them both.

Amidst a backdrop of escalating tensions between Seoul and Pyongyang, Duncan experiences the excitement, challenges and outright confusion of a foreigner living and loving in South Korea. A tale of devotion, desperation and addiction, Eight Seasons is the story of two young people deeply, perilously in love.

www.ingramcontent.com/pod-product-compliance
Lightning Source LLC
Chambersburg PA
CBHW051007060726

47593CB00017B/1105